ROB ROY
LIBRARY

Nº 9

1ᵈ⁻

THE EAGLES' NEST.

"The man climbed up the ladder, and as he gained the top he caught sight of Rob Roy ready to cut him down."

POCKET BUDGET LIBRARY

NOW ON SALE.

GRAND COMPLETE STORIES

IN ATTRACTIVE ILLUSTRATED COLOURED COVERS.

1. SONS OF THE WAVES. A Stirring Story of Fighting at Sea.
2. JACK MARLIN'S SCHOOLDAYS. A Story of Rattling Fun and Adventures at School.
3. WITH THE FUSILIERS; Or, Brothers in Arms. An Exciting Soldier Story.
4. BELTRANO THE NAMELESS; Or, The Cavaliers of Castile. A Grand Old-Time Tale of the Days of Chivalry.
5. THE PIKEMEN OF SEDGEMOOR. The Story of the Daring Adventures of Dick Seymour.
6. MIDSHIPMAN JACK MARLIN. A Splendid Story of Adventure at Sea.
7. IN THE RANKS. A Rattling Story of Adventure in India.
8. ULLAM THE UNKNOWN. A Stirring Story of the Scottish Wars.
9. LOYAL TO THE KING. A Grand Story of Remarkable Adventure.
10. DICK ASHTON OF CRANWORTH. A Rattling School Story.
11. ON THE SPANISH MAIN. Jack Marlin's Further Adventures at Sea.
12. SWORD AND CROSSBOW; Or, The Rightful Heir of Battleden.
13. WHO SERVES THE KING? A Stirring Story of Adventure in the Days of King Charles.
14. THE GRAMMAR SCHOOL BRIGADE; Or, The Rattling Adventures of Eight Schoolboys.
15. AFLOAT AND ASHORE. The Further Exciting Adventures of Lieutenant Jack Marlin.
16. THE GOLDEN KNIGHT; Or, The Secret of the Crown of Iona.
17. THE BOYS OF REDMINSTER. A School Story full of Fun and Adventures.
18. CAPTAIN JACK MARLIN. His Adventures in the Four Quarters of the Globe.
19. RUPERT, THE YOUNG SWORDSMAN. A Grand Old-Time Story.
20. FIGHTING JACK. A Thrilling Soldier Story.
21. THE SCHOOLBOY DETECTIVE. A Sequel to "The Boys of Redminster." A Grand School Tale.
22. THE LOST GALLEON. A Thrilling Story of Adventure in Search of Hidden Treasure.
23. THE DASHING DRAGOON. A Stirring War Story.
24. THE KNIGHT OF THE SILVER CROSS. A Most Exciting Old-Time Story.

EACH BOOK CONTAINS A LONG COMPLETE STORY OF ABOUT 38,000 WORDS.

Each Number Price ONE PENNY; by Post, 1½d.

FOUR SPLENDID NEW NUMBERS READY MARCH 24.

IN HIGHLY ATTRACTIVE PICTORIAL COVERS PRINTED IN COLOURS.

25. THE MYSTERY OF FARNLEIGH COLLEGE. A Splendid School Story.
26. SAVED FROM THE SEA. A Rattling Sea Story of Stirring Adventure.
27. IN THE VAN OF BATTLE. A Grand Soldier Story.
28. FENELON THE FEARLESS. An Old-Time Story full of Daring Deeds.

PLEASE ORDER AT ONCE FROM YOUR NEWSAGENT.

London: JAMES HENDERSON & SONS, Red Lion House, Red Lion Court, Fleet Street, E.C.

THE EAGLES NEST.

By ANGUS MACLEAN.

CHAPTER I.

THE SHOT-HOLED ROCK.

"STAND, or you are a dead man!"

The startling words were hissed in Rob Roy's ear as he stood beside a perpendicular rock overlooking Loch Lydoch.

Rob Roy turned quickly and faced the speaker.

"Malcolm Riach, the freebooter!" exclaimed Rob Roy.

"The same," replied the other, shortly, "and you are in my power."

He held a pair of heavy horse pistols at Rob Roy's head. He was a fierce, big, rawboned man, with long black hair and a straggling beard.

He was armed to the teeth. Across his back was slung a Spanish gun with a very long barrel. A claymore hung from his left side, while from the tops of his stockings protruded two murderous looking dirks.

Rob Roy saw that resistance was useless, and he was piqued at being surprised.

Riach seemed to spring from the rocks at his side.

"A nice beginning," thought Rob Roy, to himself. "Here I have taken in hand to rid this country of this pest, and I am caught in a trap at the very outset."

"You are in my power, Rob Roy," again hissed the freebooter through his teeth. "Prepare to meet your doom. Take off your sword-belt."

Rob Roy had looked death often in the face, and brave man that he was, he now stood his ground without flinching. At the same time there was an ugly look on Riach's face, while the ominous muzzles of the pistols covered Rob Roy's heart.

"Why should I prepare to meet my doom?" asked Rob Roy, boldly.

"Why ask such a question?" demanded Riach, fiercely. "Have you not told the Macphersons that you will take care that I will trouble them no more?"

"I have," replied Rob Roy, quietly, "and I mean it."

"Take off your sword-belt, and lay your claymore on the ground."

"Why trouble about my claymore when I have but a few minutes to live."

"Minutes!" roared Riach, pulling both triggers, "second, you mean. Die!"

There was a blinding flash and Rob Roy felt the fiery blast on his face and neck. He had given himself up for lost, but a curious thing had happened. Instead of being shot, Rob Roy stood stock still while a yell arose from behind, and in front of him Riach was knocked head over heels with an arrow sticking through his shoulder.

Rob Roy sprang at him through the smoke, but Riach was on his feet and disappeared as if by magic.

At that moment several men, rough-looking fellows in deer-skin leggings and thick woollen doublets, ran towards Rob Roy.

Rob Roy turned.

"Davidson of Glenshee!" he exclaimed, heartily. "What lucky chance brought you here?"

"Lucky for you, Rob," replied the smuggler, for smuggler he was; "I managed to pink him just in time. I was afraid I was late, and I had to take my chance, for your body was in the way of a straight shot."

"I am in your debt once more," said Rob Roy, shaking Davidson heartily by the hand. "It was a good shot, but I don't often see you with a bow and arrow."

"No, that you don't. The claymore and pistol are more in my line, but it so happens that arrows are the best for this part of the country."

"Indeed," replied Rob Roy, in surprise; "how is that?"

"For this reason. You see that rock towering straight up," said Davidson, pointing to a perpendicular mass of rock that rose sheer out of the hill-side.

"Yes, I do."

"Do you know what they call it?"

"No," replied Rob Roy. "As a matter of fact, I have come to explore this part of the country and clear it of Malcolm Riach, the freebooter."

"You have your work cut out. But as I was saying, that rock is called the Eagles' Nest. There is an eyrie there, and besides there is something peculiar about it."

"How so?"

"Well, if you look closely at the face of the rock you will notice it dotted with holes. That is said to be loopholes made by Riach."

"To shoot people from?"

"Yes. You see the rock overlooks the roadway, but, examine the rock how you like, you cannot see any entrance or any means of entrance that Riach may have, that is if he really uses the rock."

"That is very strange."

"It is. The people about here say they have seen the smoke from the shot-holes, but in any case, when passing near the rock, I always have an arrow ready. You see you may be concealed, and there being no smoke, your position is not given away to anyone watching you."

"And are there eagles in the eyrie?"

"Yes. You can see them any time. Folk also say that the Eagles' Nest is Riach's stronghold, but I don't know."

"Well," said Rob Roy, "I shall soon have to know, and I mean to find out.

I must admit there is something peculiar, for the moment I had arrived here and stood by the rock, Riach appeared from goodness knows where, pointing a pair of pistols at me."

"I have heard of that custom of his. He does not stop at murder if anything is to be had," said Davidson, "and I believe he is very partial to our whisky; but when I come along I'm ready for him."

"And a mercy it was you came along to-day," said Rob Roy. "Look out!"

An arrow hissed vengefully between them as they spoke.

"That's from one of the shot-holes of the rock," laughed Davidson. "He has got the range, so I vote we move on a little."

CHAPTER II.

A HAUNTED SPOT.

Suiting the action to the word, Davidson turned on his heel and ordered his men to the carts.

But as he turned he uttered an exclamation of surprise.

When he and his men had run forward on seeing Rob Roy's danger, they left their carts, loaded with smuggled spirit, standing on the roadway some fifty yards off.

The carts were hidden from view by one of the huge bulging rocks that overhung the road. But when he turned and advanced a few paces he saw that the carts were gone.

Not the slightest trace of them was anywhere, and to increase their surprise a blazing carcass—a wooden hollow ball filled with Greek fire—burst in their midst with a loud report.

The spluttering flames fortunately spread over one man only. Maddened by the fierce burning he rushed towards the loch.

Rob Roy sprang towards him and enveloped him with his plaid, beating the flames out.

The man struggled forward.

"Back, man!" shouted Rob Roy. "Don't go near the water. It is Greek fire and will burn all the more fiercely."

"Let us go," said Davidson, "the place is haunted. I have always heard so. That man is a devil."

"Lend a hand. Davidson!" exclaimed Rob Roy, as he examined the smuggler's wounds, while his comrades took to their heels and ran. "They might be worse, my man," said Rob Roy; "your beard is singed off, but, thanks to your deerskin doublet, you have escaped injury."

"I am not hurt," said the smuggler, in a low voice, "but for God's sake let me run from this enchanted place. I fear no man, but I will not fight the pixies."

Saying so, he tore himself away and rushed after his comrades.

"A nice state of affairs, I'm thinking," muttered Davidson. "What do you think of it, Rob Roy? The sooner I get along to Dalmally the better."

"But what about your carts?"

"I clean forgot about them!" exclaimed Davidson, with a groan, "and we were reckoning on the sale of the spirits to keep us going through the winter."

"Never mind," replied Rob Roy, consolingly, "we shall find them."

"They are spirited away," groaned Davidson. For, despite his great courage and bravery, he was very superstitious.

"They are certainly spirits," laughed Rob Roy, "and overproof at that. Come, let us look for them."

As they walked along they found the smugglers gathered together in a silent group.

"They have been spirited away," said one, addressing Davidson.

"What did I tell you, Rob," exclaimed Davidson, turning to Rob Roy.

"Stuff and nonsense," replied Rob Roy, with emphasis; "the carts were here not twenty minutes ago, and they have got to be found. Show me the exact spot where they were."

"Here," said Davidson, "four of them all in a row. We pulled them over the heather ourselves from Dalnaspidal, where we left the horses. They could not cross the pass of Drumochter."

Rob Roy examined the ground carefully, but no track was left, for the heather was thick all round.

"It stands to reason that one man alone could not move them. How many men have you for each?"

"We are nine," replied Davidson. "Two men to each cart and myself."

"Then it would certainly have taken six men to move them."

"No man moved them," replied the smugglers in chorus, "it was the pixies."

Rob Roy could have laughed, but he did not wish to offend the men. They were deeply in earnest.

The place was a bleak one. The silent loch by their side, the black mysterious rock towering above it, and nothing between the encircling hills and themselves but bare purple heather.

"Come along, men," said Rob Roy, cheerily. "Let us commence the search. A man cannot put a cart and a couple of barrels of whisky in his sporran."

The smugglers shook their heads.

"Better leave them with the fairies, Rob Roy," said one man, advancing. He was a tall, strapping fellow, but his face showed unmistakable signs of dread.

"Do as Rob Roy tells you, Big John," said Davidson.

But Big John, or Ian Mohr, as his comrades called him, apparently had no intention of doing so.

"Ian Mohr," said Rob Roy, "the carts are better with us. You will admit that?"

"Yes; but we cannot get them, Rob Roy. I tell you," he said, with intensity, "we cannot get them. The whole valley is haunted!"

"Haunted?" queried Rob Roy. "What do you know about it?"

"I was born not many miles from here," replied Big John, below his breath, as if afraid to anger the fairies, "and I know it is haunted. Did not Dougal Macintosh try to get back the sheep that strayed into the glen, and was not his body found torn to pieces?"

"By what?" asked Rob Roy.

"By the eagles, it was said. They say," continued Big John, lowering his voice, "that the eagles of the nest are evil spirits."

Rob Roy burst into a hearty laugh, while the smugglers looked at him in dismay.

"'Tis all very well for you, Rob Roy, to laugh," replied Big John, deprecatingly. "You are the chief of a powerful clan from the South, but we here are few and far between, and with my own eyes I have seen the ghosts."

"Ghosts?" queried Rob Roy.

"Ay, ghosts!" interjected Davidson. "Big John speaks truly, for I have seen them myself."

"And I have seen," exclaimed Big John, "a spectre walking over the loch at night, and I have seen that black rock twinkle in the darkness, and heard the mocking laughter of the evil one!"

And Big John pointed fearsomely to the towering rock of the Eagles' Nest.

"There was some reason for it,"

replied Rob Roy, thoughtfully, as he looked at the earnest and awed face of Big John.

"There was no reason. It was the Black Art. If any human being had a hand in it," replied Big John, "he is in league with the evil one."

"That may be so," said Rob Roy, "but I am going to find out!"

"Not me," said Big John.

"Not me," replied the others in chorus.

"I'll give you a hand," exclaimed Davidson; "but if we do not find the carts soon, we must go back to Dalnaspidal and thence towards Glenshee for another supply."

"Very well," said Rob Roy. "Let your men remain here by the roadway while we explore. If you see anything, men, give the alarm at once."

"For the past year," said Davidson, as he and Rob Roy moved off, "there have been no fewer than seven brutal murders—every one of them a Macpherson."

"Is it because they are Macphersons?" asked Rob Roy, "or is it because they live in the vicinity?"

"As to that I cannot tell," replied Davidson; "but this I do know, they were murdered. On that account for miles around you cannot get a Macpherson to open their doors after dark."

"What are they afraid of?"

"The ghosts."

"But the ghosts did not murder them?"

"That I cannot tell, only this: The district is haunted, and not a soul will live in it. Malcolm Riach, as he is called, is known to have taken up his abode here; some say on the Eagles' Nest Rock, others say in some hiding-place on the hills."

"Then he is the murderer!" replied Roy Roy, emphatically, "and is in hiding, and I shall rout him out!"

They seached high and low for the missing carts, but no trace of them could they see.

"Let us go back to the roadway," said Rob Roy, "and commence over again. The heather has been burnt some time ago for the express purpose of covering up the tracks of any who may pass this way. Had the heather been long, we should have seen the traces of the wheels at once."

As he spoke a shadow passed overhead.

Davidson started. "There they are! There they are!" he shouted, pointing upwards.

"Who?" asked Rob Roy, looking up. "Oh, the eagles!" he added, as he saw two huge birds wheeling in circles overhead.

In a moment they became motionless, and then dropped like falling stones to the eyrie on the black rock.

Rob Roy watched them.

"I should like to be able to climb that distance," he muttered.

"It is impossible," replied Davidson, who overheard him. "For the rock bulges out on all sides half way up."

"I see that," said Rob Roy; "but what I have been thinking of was the burning shot. It was fired from a mortar from the Eagles' Nest, but how on earth it got there is beyond my comprehension."

"And the carts," said Davidson, ruefully.

"And the carts," repeated Rob Roy. "Now let us see. The hills are in the distance. The carts could not be taken there without our seeing them; for although the ground is very rough and broken, it is not uneven enough to hide them."

"And another thing is," said Davidson, "that they could not have been hauled over this rocky stretch," and he pointed to a long line of jumbled rocks that ran from the water side to the distant hills.

"But," urged Rob Roy, "your carts were drawn up alongside of the same stretch."

"That is so," replied Davidson.

"Well," said Rob Roy, decidedly, "they must be near. We shall search the rocks."

CHAPTER III.
AT BAY.

No sooner had Rob Roy and Davidson commenced the search than half-a-dozen bullets flattened themselves on the rocks beside them.

"That means we are on the right track," exclaimed Rob Roy, as he looked towards the Eagles' Nest. A few feet below the eyrie itself a thick plume of smoke was oozing out slowly.

"There is a gang, Davidson, for certain," exclaimed Rob Roy.

As he spoke another volley rattled

about their heads, and the eagles rose screaming from the eyrie.

"Rather close work," said Davidson, as he shook the blood from his left hand, the back of which was grazed by a bullet.

"Are you hurt?" asked Rob Roy, observing Davidson's motion.

"Nothing to speak of; but all the same we should be safer under cover. I don't mind the bullets, but I object to being a target without a chance of hitting back."

"Discretion is the better part of valour," replied Rob Roy, "and a live dog is better than a dead lion. We have at least found out that they object to us searching this stretch of rocky ground. Let us rejoin the men."

"Go and search everywhere," ordered Davidson, as he and Rob Roy reached the smugglers. "Only I may warn you to keep well under cover if you venture on the rocky ground."

"So you haven't found the carts," said Big John. "I knew you wouldn't."

"In good time, Ian Mohr," replied Rob Roy. "No doubt they are somewhere among these rocks, but in daylight we shall not be able to get near them."

"What would you propose doing," asked Davidson of Rob Roy.

"Simply this that I shall keep watch to-night. I am quite certain it is useless to do anything during the day. We would simply be shot down."

"If we can help you, Rob Roy, you may rely on us," said Davidson.

"That I well know," replied Rob Roy, "but I intend to watch by myself. If we all stayed we should be sure to betray ourselves."

"I shall stay with you, Rob Roy," said Davidson, "for I should not sleep all night thinking of you in this perilous position."

"No, old friend," replied Rob Roy, firmly. "I thank you very much, but it is best that I should be alone, and besides, you must not be drawn into this quarrel."

"Drawn into the quarrel," laughed Davidson. "Surely when I drew my bow I drew myself very much into it."

Rob Roy burst into a hearty laugh.

"It was a strong draw," exclaimed Rob Roy.

"And a stronger draw for Riach, or whatever he calls himself, when he took

the carts," returned Davidson, "if he did take them."

"He did," replied Rob Roy. "I have no patience with all this nonsense about fairies and witches."

"So I said at one time," interrupted Davidson; "but I have seen and heard things which go beyond me, and for that reason I insist that I shall stay by you."

"So be it," said Rob Roy, resignedly. "But what about the men?"

"We shall stay if required," answered Big John. "We do not care to fight evil spirits in the dark, but we care more for you."

"Well said!" exclaimed Rob Roy, "but I think, Davidson, that you and I will be sufficient."

"Yes," replied Davidson, turning to the smugglers. "You better make yourselves comfortable for the night on the hills beyond, and be ready by morning's light."

CHAPTER IV.

A NIGHT VIGIL.

Although they discussed their plans in the shadow of the rocks, Rob Roy knew that they were being watched by unseen eyes.

He, therefore, determined to make a pretence of marching away.

"Let us make for the distant hills," said Rob Roy, "then you and I, Davidson can return under cover of darkness."

Accordingly they marched off, and did not once look round until they reached the hills. Entering a narrow glen, the men flung themselves on the heather, where they were to pass the night, while Rob Roy and Davidson patiently awaited the coming of darkness.

As soon as the night became pitch black, Rob Roy and Davidson silently stole from the glen in the mountains.

"Let us keep to the left," whispered Rob Roy, "so that the heather may deaden our footfall." "And keep away from the rocks. We should lose ourselves in the darkness," said Davidson, below his breath.

"The loch is straight ahead and when we reach it the Eagles' Nest is about fifty paces to the right," said Rob Roy.

"Lord defend us!" exclaimed Davidson, seizing Rob Roy's arm. "What's that?"

Rob Roy peered through the darkness at a strange sight.

In front of them—how far they could

not tell—the phantom figure of a man in a boat gradually divulged itself.

He was surrounded by rolling flames of fire, through which he could be seen standing in the stern of the boat, sculling with an oar.

Every movement of the oar stirred up tongues of sulphurous flame. All around was intensely black. It was an awesome sight, and not a sound broke the stillness of the night.

"It is the evil one," whispered Davidson, with a shudder.

"Hush!" whispered Rob Roy, who was intently watching the fearsome phantom. "Wait. He is on the loch."

Throwing himself flat on the ground and pressing his ear close to it, he lay like a log.

"He is disappearing," whispered Davidson, in awe-struck tones, as Rob Roy sprang to his feet.

The phantom became shadowy and finally disappeared.

"Yes," said Rob Roy, "I felt his boat graze on the shingle. It is too far to hear. Come on."

Shuddering involuntarily, Davidson followed Rob Roy, who strode swiftly onwards.

They soon came to the edge of the loch.

"It is terrible," muttered Davidson. "A man has only once to die, and I shall die sword in hand."

"Don't speak," whispered Rob Roy, "there is no mystery, I have seen the same at Loch Maree and in the sea at Skye. See!"

Quickly bending down Rob Roy picked up a flat piece of slatey stone and threw it from him.

Four sparks of phosphorescent light burst from the darkness, followed by a long streak of rolling, shadowy fire.

Rob Roy heard Davidson breathe heavily.

"Listen," whispered Rob Roy, drawing Davidson close to him and speaking in his ear. "There is no mystery. It is a phosphorescent loch, common in the west. The phantom was a man and every time he moved his oar he stirred up the phosphorus in the water. He is one of the gang of murderers. When he took his oar out of the water the illusion ceased. Follow me, I have seen the sea in Loch Alsh in flames."

"Wait," again whispered Rob Roy, as he bent down and took off his shoes, "we must keep on the roadway."

There was no necessity for Davidson to use special precaution for the coverings of his feet were made of soft deerskin and created no noise on the hard ground.

Silently and swiftly the two pressed forward. Although they could not see it, they felt the huge black rock of the Eagles' Nest towering above them.

"Let us try and find the boat," whispered Rob Roy, "keep close to the edge of the water."

"Hist, here it is."

Suddenly there came a blinding flash of light.

"Lightning," said Davidson.

"Hist," whispered Rob Roy.

Hollow footsteps sounded in the vicinity.

"Someone is approaching us," whispered Rob Roy.

Both listened intently. They could hear the beating of their own hearts. The footsteps were close at hand, but from what direction they proceeded they could not tell. As is usual in the darkness, they sounded sometimes behind, sometimes in front, and sometimes from all the different points of the compass together.

Suddenly a heavy body bumped against Rob Roy. It was a man, and Rob Roy grappled with him, but he slipped through Rob Roy's arms.

Davidson sprang forward. There was an oath, a scrimmage, and a groan, as Davidson staggered backwards stabbed by a dagger thrust in the left arm.

In the confusion the man escaped. They could hear his rapid footfall on the pebbles.

"He was making for the boat," whispered Rob Roy, "but it is useless to follow in this darkness. Are you much hurt?"

"Only a stab in the arm."

"The boat must be destroyed," said Rob Roy, feeling about for it in the inky blackness.

"Knock the plug out," said Davidson, "then, in the morning we shall carry the boat off."

"Good idea," replied Rob Roy, "hold the boat until I board it."

Finding the plug, Rob Roy seized an oar and knocked it out."

As he lightly leapt ashore the boat rapidly filled with water.

"That will do," muttered Rob Roy, as he handed the other oar to Davidson, "we might as well take them with us."

CHAPTER V.

BAFFLED.

" What shall we do ? " asked Davidson.

" Let us retire for about twenty paces and wait for the rising of the moon," said Rob Roy.

" That is about midnight," said Davidson.

" Yes," replied Rob Roy, " we cannot do anything till then."

When they had retired some distance, they sat down on the soft heather under the rocks facing the loch. Not a sound broke the solemn silence.

" There is some mystery attached to this spot," whispered Rob Roy. " Why does Riach resort to all this tomfoolery ? Why does he invest the glen with a spirit of sorcery ? And why have these horrible murders been committed. Surely not for the sake of mere robbery ? "

" Ay," said Davidson, " why ? It is a most curious thing for one man to be able to terrorise the country if he is not helped by the evil one."

" He is helped by good flesh and blood," replied Rob Roy, " and he has some reason for mystifying the people, and that reason I am going to find out."

Davidson did not answer. He was deep in thought. Rob Roy soon commenced the whispered conversation.

" What do you know of this Riach ? " he asked.

" Nothing at all," replied Davidson, " or practically nothing at all. It is said he is a foreigner, and that he settled among the Macphersons."

" He is not a foreigner," replied Rob Roy. " I know him of old. He belongs to the clan Ross."

" A bad lot," interjected Davidson, and always will be.

" Do you remember," asked Rob Roy, " when the *Atlanta* was wrecked off the Ballachulish coast ? "

" I do," replied Davidson, " a year ago come next month."

" The very same," said Rob Roy; " and you remember that it was said she was run ashore on purpose."

" I heard something of that," returned Davidson.

" And the killing of the Macphersons commenced after that time ? " queried Rob Roy.

" I believe you are right," said Davidson, " but what has the murder of the Macphersons to do with this work of the evil one ? "

" Everything," replied Rob Roy. " I have got an idea."

" That is more than I have," said Davidson, " for I am puzzled."

For a long time neither spoke. At last Rob Roy broke the silence.

" How is it," he whispered, " that the clan Macpherson have not tried to avenge these murders ? "

" Because the clan is away up north in Invernesshire, and the Macphersons about here are only some dozen families that quarrelled with the chief and settled here."

" And it has been the head of each family that has been murdered ? "

" Yes. There are only the women and the children left, and they are wondering why their husbands came south."

" And they settled here over a year ago ? " queried Rob Roy.

" Yes," answered Davidson, with a shudder, " to come to their death."

For a long time the two lay in silence, and at last the grey dawn began to show on the horizon.

" Not much good watching much longer," said Davidson, rising and stretching his cramped limbs.

" Wait for another half hour," said Rob. " Perhaps with daybreak some one may be stirring."

But with daybreak there was no sign of a human being. The gunwale of the submerged boat showed plainly above the water, and as the sun burst forth in all his glory, the eagles rose screaming from their eyrie.

" We must give it up as a bad job," said Davidson. " I must be going, for I must hurry back home for another supply of spirits. I must be quick, too, for delivery is promised in three days' time."

" Let us have another try to find the carts," said Rob Roy. " I don't like the idea of giving up the search yet."

" Nor do I, but time presses. When I return I shall give you a hand."

" Many thanks, Davidson, but I have made up my plans. I am to return to the Braes of Balquhidder, and then I shall commence the campaign. We may meet here again as I come north and you go south."

" So be it," returned Davidson. " We will go and wake the men."

The smugglers sprang from the heather, shaking the dew off their plaids, on Davidson's shout.

"Come on, men, back to Glenshee with all speed. We'll get something to eat at Rannoch."

"Good-bye, and God speed you, Rob Roy," said Davidson, shaking Rob Roy's hand.

"Good speed you, Rob Roy," shouted the smugglers, lifting their bonnets and giving a hearty cheer.

CHAPTER VI.

A Tangled Web.

There was a scene of excitement amongst the remnant of the exciled Macphersons as they stood at the doors of the six cottages that formed the colony.

These rudely-constructed cottages stood in a sequestered nook amongst the bleak mountains that overlook Glencoe.

The exiles were only women and children who had fled in dismay from their small village by the banks of Loch Lydoch.

At the present moment they stood shading their eyes with their hands, looking intently down the hillside at an approaching figure of a man.

He was of gigantic stature, and walked up the hillside with a graceful ease.

"He's a Macpherson," shouted Eppie Macpherson, the oldest woman of the exiles. "He's a Macpherson!" she repeated in excited tones.

"What a handsome man!" exclaimed one of the younger women as the stranger gained the plateau on which the cottages stood.

"I know him not," muttered old Eppie. "But he wears the Macpherson tartan."

"He'll be one of the Tulloch Macphersons," said the younger woman.

"Aye, may be," replied Eppie.

At that moment the stranger lifted his bonnet and approached.

"Good morn to ye, ladies!" he exclaimed in a cheery voice, a smile lighting up his handsome features.

"Good morn to ye, sir," replied the women, curtseying with true Highland politeness.

"You've been having troublous times, good wife," he said, addressing Eppie.

"That we have, and may we be preserved from more."

"Amen, so let it be," responded the stranger.

"Come in, sir!" exclaimed Eppie. "We have not much to offer, but, such as it is, you are welcome."

The stranger seated himself by the peat fire after the women had sat down, with the children clinging to their skirts.

"What news bring you?" asked Eppie

"Not much, to tell you the truth," was the reply. "The clan is doing well, but I came more for information."

"What we know we shall tell," replied Eppie; "and what we know is bitter truth."

The stranger inclined his head.

"I have heard of your sufferings, and it would ill become a Highlander to turn a deaf ear," was his noble response.

"Has the chief sent you here?" asked Eppie.

"No," replied the stranger.

"Then he has left us to our fate?" queried Eppie, in tones of sadness.

"I do not think the chief knows of your trouble, but I am determined to put it before him. But why not return? The clan will welcome you with open arms."

"Oh, no!" replied Eppie. "We know the chief. We left in anger."

"Then why did you leave?"

"You a Macpherson, and not know that!"

"I do not know, and there are many who do not know. I am asking for information, as I said before."

"What the quarrel was I do not know. Our men—all, alas! dead—never told us why we left, except that they said it was for our good."

"Then your good men knew the reason?" queried the stranger.

"Indeed they did," interrupted the young woman, already mentioned. "Indeed they did, for they held secret meetings."

"Secret meetings?"

"Yes, secret meetings, and much did I grudge the time they took my Fergus from me. Now, alas! he is dead!"

"And did Fergus never tell you anything?" asked the stranger, feelingly.

"I asked him often," replied the young woman; "but his only answer was 'Some day I will tell you.'"

"Fergus was my son," explained Eppie, "and Janet here is my daughter-in-law. We are all related."

"Sons of yours?" hazarded the stranger.

"Yes," replied Eppie, sadly. "My seven sons and their families!"

"I was told there were a dozen families."

"That is wrong. Seven is the number, and seven murders have left us mourning!"

"But what was the quarrel?" asked the stranger.

"Did you ever hear of Fergus of the Sea?" answered Eppie, asking another question in the Scotch fashion in reply to the query.

"Fergus Macpherson, the Highland sailor of the Spanish schooner *Atlanta?*" asked the stranger, with a start.

"The very same," said Eppie.

"I knew him," was the unexpected reply. "I met him once in Glasgow. He was set upon by roughs, who tried to take his hard-earned money. I was passing, and he shouted for help in Gaelic, which made me move all the quicker, I can tell you. We drove them off, but he was stabbed in the face."

As the stranger spoke, the entire company gazed hard at him.

In an instant old Eppie sprang to her feet in great excitement.

"I know ye now—my son's preserver! You are no Macpherson, but the noble chieftain of the Clan Gregor!"

And, rushing towards him, old Eppie embraced the gallant cheiftain before he had time to rise.

"It is Rob Roy! It is the noble MacGregor!" shouted the women; and the children stared at the renowned chief in wide-eyed wonder.

When Rob Roy had disengaged himself from Eppie's embrace, he sat thoughtfully for a while.

"I am Rob Roy," he said, with a laugh, "and evidently over-valued. I was only too glad to be of assistance to Fergus."

"Assistance!" echoed Fergus's wife, gazing at Rob Roy in admiration. "Assistance! Why, you should have heard Fergus speak of you. One hundred times he has said, if it had not been for you, he would have been a dead man."

Rob Roy shook his head disparagingly.

"No, no," he said; "but let that pass."

"But why wear the Macpherson tartan?" asked Effie.

"I have a plan," replied Rob Roy, "which I cannot yet explain, and which is merely a jump in the dark. I landed at Ballachulish, and every one in the village saw that a Macpherson had arrived."

"Another Macpherson come to his death," said one of the fishermen.

"I passed by," continued Rob Roy, "and I want one of you or some of the boys to go to Ballachulish as if to buy something, and when questioned to say that Peter Macpherson has come to take up his abode by the banks of Loch Lydoch."

The women shuddered.

"But you'll not do that?" they exclaimed aghast.

"Not at present, but I want it to be known."

"God preserve you and us," muttered Eppie; "we know, Rob Roy, that you are a noble and fearless man, but it is tempting Providence."

"But," she added, as the pride of her clan rose in her breast, "You not being a Macpherson, you may escape the curse."

Rob Roy did not answer. He was thinking.

"I have not had time to explore the vicinity of the rock," he said at length. "How many empty houses are there?"

"Seven," replied Effie, with a shudder.

"And six of them are red with blood."

"Were the six killed in their houses?"

"Yes; stabbed to the heart in the dead of the night."

"And the seventh?"

"Disappeared from the face of the earth."

"Who was he?"

"Fergus. He was the first to go. We never found his body."

"And the others were stabbed at home?"

"Yes," replied Eppie.

"And no alarm given?"

"There was no alarm, and no blood spilt," replied Eppie enigmatically.

"No blood spilt?" exclaimed Rob Roy, in surprise.

"No," replied Eppie. "In the morning we found our men dead. At first we could not believe it; we could see no wound, but when we looked closer we saw to our horror a glass dagger, broken off at the hilt, sticking in their breasts.

"Only a reddish spot marked the place, but no blood was spilt until we pulled the daggers out."

"An Italian has a hand in this," muttered Rob Roy. Then loudly, "Were they all murdered in one night?"

"No, no," replied Eppie. "They all occurred during the past four months, all except Fergus, and that was a year ago. When our last man died we fled."

"Fergus was a sailor," continued Eppie, "and when he came home two years ago he was full of strange tales of the sea. We Highland folk had never seen the sea; but, anyway, after Fergus came home, his brothers grew discontented. Then Fergus went to sea once more, promising to return in a year's time. The ship was lost on the coast."

"And Fergus was safe?" asked Rob Roy.

"Not altogether. There was a mutiny on board. Fergus was attacked because he stood by the captain, and when the captain was shot he sprang overboard and swam ashore."

"After that," continued Eppie, "the boat was run on the rocks, and more than that Fergus did not know, for he made straight for home. He gave up the sea, and he and his brothers, who had been expecting him, left the clan."

"Why?" asked Rob Roy.

"I do not know; only that the chief was angry and ordered them never to show their faces again."

"And on that account," said Rob Roy, "you are afraid to return?"

"We are," was the reply from all.

"And if you could return, would you?" asked Rob Roy.

"We would," replied all the women in a breath.

"Then," said Rob Roy, "I am going to see your chief. I shall put the matter before him, and it will not be my blame if you are not soon under the protection of the clan once more."

"Thank you, noble MacGregor," exclaimed Eppie, "but I am afraid your task is hopeless."

"No task," gallantly replied Rob Roy. "It is a pleasure. And if the chief's heart is hardened, then I shall take you to my clan. You cannot remain unprotected like this."

"Now," continued Rob Roy, "I must start at once, and meantime, you spread it abroad that another Macpherson is taking up his abode by Loch Lydoch. My home," he added, laughingly, "will be a good ten miles from here, but by then I hope you will be back to your clan."

"God bless you and keep you safe," murmured the women as they stood at the doors of the cottages waving farewell to the gallant chieftain as he strode down the mountain side.

CHAPTER VII.

THE CHIEFTAIN'S STORY.

When Rob Roy reached the foot of the hill, he turned his face in the direction of Loch Lydoch.

With a swinging stride he covered the intervening ten miles, and soon the ominous rock of the Eagles' Nest loomed black on the horizon.

As he approached he kept his eye on it steadfastly, but all he saw was the male eagle circling round and round it.

Coming nearer to the loch he struck to the right, and in a few minutes he came upon the seven deserted houses.

They presented a melancholy spectacle. Roy Roy listened intently in case an enemy might be about, but he heard no sound.

Slinging the bundle he carried over his shoulder, and fastening it to his sword belt, he drew one of his pistols with his left hand, at the same time pulling his claymore from its sheath with his right.

Thus armed, he advanced cautiously to the nearest house and pushed the door open. The house consisted of one room. It was bare. Not a sound broke the silence.

Rob Roy gazed around and saw a dark stain on the wall and on the floor.

"The withdrawal of the stiletto caused that," muttered Rob Roy. "Poor women! what a time it must have been for them!"

He examined the ground carefully in case of a hidden trap-door, but nothing could he see.

Advancing to the end of the room, he looked up the chimney. "Wide enough," he muttered, "to let a dozen men down."

The door, he observed, had no bolt or lock, only a wooden beam having been used to lean against it to keep it shut.

"No difficulty there for an assassin," he thought.

When Rob Roy was satisfied that no one was about, he stuck his pistol in his belt, but did not sheath his sword. He stuck it in the earthen floor ready for use at a moment's notice.

Taking the bundle from his back he undid it, and in a twinkling exchanged the Macpherson dress for his own clothes of MacGregor tartan. Placing an eagle's plume in his bonnet as a sign of his chieftainship, he bundled up his Macpherson tartan kilt and secreting it in the wide chimney, left the house.

"Now," he muttered, "to see the chief of the Macphersons."

Rob Roy turned his face towards the north, and commenced his arduous journey to the territory of the Macphersons.

Night overtook him before he had gone many miles, and wrapping his plaid around him, he was soon fast asleep on the heather.

Next morning at sunrise he was well on his journey, and by afternoon arrived at Macpherson's castle.

Advancing to the gateway he blew a long blast on the horn.

"Who calls?" shouted the seneschal behind the raised drawbridge.

"The MacGregor," was the answer.

"What want ye?" challenged the man.

"The Macpherson."

"On what business?"

"Sufficient that the MacGregor calls," was the proud reply.

The seneschal retired muttering, and after a few minutes' absence reappeared.

With rattling chains the draw-bridge was let down. "Enter," said the seneschal. "The Macpherson will see you."

Rob Roy was conducted to the room of the chief of the Macphersons.

He was a fine-looking old man, tall of stature, with silver hair.

"Welcome, MacGregor," he said cordially, as he extended his hand. "It is not often we have your company in these parts."

"The more to my loss," replied Rob Roy, genially.

"Well, well," said Macpherson, "make yourself at home, and first of all have something to eat."

Blowing a whistle, made out of a deer's foot, the Macpherson gave orders to the servant, who appeared in answer to the summons, to prepare a meal.

When Rob Roy had done justice to it, Macpherson said, "And now, Rob Roy, I am at your service. What would you?"

"You remember the members of your clan who left a year ago?"

"Yes. They left on a wild goose chase. I told them so."

"It has been a wild goose chase for them."

"How so?"

"Because all the men are dead—murdered!"

"Murdered!" exclaimed Macpherson, rising from his chair in horror and astonishment, "murdered!"

"Yes, murdered," replied Rob Roy.

"There must be more in it than what I thought," said Macpherson, as if speaking to himself.

"More in what?" asked Rob Roy.

"Oh! I was thinking," replied Macpherson, with a start, "I was thinking. But you surprise me."

"It is said," answered Rob Roy, "that you drove them from the clan in anger?"

"Who dare say such a thing?" demanded Macpherson.

"That is the story I heard, anyway," returned Rob Roy.

"They were not driven away in anger. They went of their own free will, and I was angry for their going. The family was one of the best of the clan."

"Then why did they leave?"

"Ay! that's the question, why? Until Fergus Macpherson returned home from sea they were quite contented."

"And," interjected Rob Roy, "it was something he said or did that caused the disruption."

"You have no idea," replied Macpherson, "what a commotion the return of Fergus caused. You see, in the central Highlands our people had hazy notions of the sea. Many had never seen it, and certainly the only sailor of the clan was Fergus.

"He told them wondrous tales?"

"He did, and he unfolded a peculiar one to me."

"Does it bear repetition?"

"There is no reason why, and the events you tell me of make me think the affair is not a fancy of a disordered brain."

Rob Roy listened eagerly.

"I am all ears," he said. "It was to hear this tale that I came here."

"The story is this," continued Macpherson. "Fergus was a wild lad, and ran off to Glasgow, where he shipped to sea. After many years knocking about he returned home. The people listened to him open-mouthed, but there was one thing he did not tell them of, and that was a mystic chart he brought with him."

" A mystic chart ? " queried Rob Roy.

" Yes," returned Macpherson, " listen! He came to me with this chart. It was written in French, and on it was rough drawing of a rock, marked ' Eagles' Nest,' beside some water. On the opposite side of the paper was a diagram of a compass with a long arrow pointing north-east. At the end of the arrow were the words ' 50 paces.' "

" At the foot of the chart was indecipherable writing, faded with rough usage and time. I tried to make it out, but could only distinguish ' Expeditionary Force.' "

" And what was it then ? "

" According to Fergus, the chart marked the spot where treasure was buried."

" Buried treasure in the Highlands ? " laughed Rob Roy.

" That's what I said at once, but his story was rather convincing."

" Indeed ! "

" Yes ! I questioned him how he came by the chart, and he told me that the vessel he was on was wrecked on the French coast, and he and another sailor, Donetto, an Italian, were the only ones saved."

" They were washed ashore, and hardly had they recovered than they heard cries for help. It was dusk, I ought to have told you, and when Fergus and his companion rushed forward to where the sounds proceeded from they could discern a noble-looking old man defending himself with a walking stick against three rough-looking fellows."

" They were footpads, and fled on the approach of Fergus and Donetto. The old man was extremely grateful, and when he discovered that Fergus came from Scotland he was extremely interested."

" I know your county well," he said. " When you come to my house I shall show you something of interest."

" Fergus and Donnetto accompanied the old fellow—an old soldier—to his house, and were treated very well. Soon after their arrival, after a great deal of searching in an old box, the Frenchman produced the chart. His father was Colonel D'etlang, who was paymaster of the expeditionary force that had left France some seventy years ago to go to the help of the King of Scotland."

" This force, the old man explained, had the worst of luck. Intending to make for Skye, they first were wrecked in the Firth of Lorn, the captain of the vessel having lost his reckoning. Then, in attempting to march by land, they got lost amongst the awful hills. They were starving, and despaired of ever leaving the hills alive, and in their last extremity they buried their treasure-chest by a huge loch by the side of a loch.

" The force, devoid of transport, then pushed forward, and a remnant reached the coast in a destitute condition. Colonel D'etlang made the chart, and determined to attempt to recover the treasure at the first opportunity. Soon a vessel took them to France, but on the way they again endured terrible privation, and Colonel D'etlang returned to France to die. The chart he left with his son, who was then but a boy."

" The boy grew up to manhood, and made two separate attempts to find the treasure, but without success. Then he gave it up, thrust the chart in an old chest, went to the wars, came home a veteran, and did not remember anything about the chart until he learned that Fergus was a Scotchman."

" A most wonderful story," replied Rob Roy, who was thinking deeply. " It makes the way more clear, and my suspicions are confirmed."

" What suspicions ? "

" About the murders of the Macphersons."

" I don't see it has anything to do with it."

" But you have not finished the story. What about the chart."

" Oh ! by the way, the old Frenchman presented it specially to Fergus, with the laughing remark that if he ever found the treasure he might keep it."

" And Donetto was there ? "

" Yes, by Saint Andrew," exclaimed Macpherson, " and that explains the other part of the story I know."

" What is that ? "

" Fergus and Donetto afterwards found a ship that took them to London, and when talking over this chart

Fergus suddenly remembered that when walking from here to Glasgow he passed a rock with an eagles' nest on it."

"And I expect he told Donetto so," interjected Rob Roy.

"Yes, and Donetto became very friendly with him. They shipped on the same vessel, the *Atlanta*, which made for Glasgow. Fergus went home and returned on board. Twice his life was attempted by someone—always in the dark, and once he was attacked in France, whither he had gone only to find that the old Frenchman was dead. To cut the story short, a mutiny occurred on board the *Atlanta*, and the mutineers steered the vessel for Loch Lynne."

"For Ballachulish, no doubt," said Rob Roy, "as the nearest point to Loch Lydoch."

"When they entered the loch the mutineers made a desperate attack on the captain and those who stood by him, amongst whom was Fergus. Ultimately they shot the captain and a few of the men, and to save his life Fergus jumped overboard. Then he came home and gave up the sea."

"Only to return to Loch Lydoch to be murdered," said Rob Roy.

"It is a terrible story," murmured Macpherson. "What about the women and children?" he asked, anxiously.

"They are safe but destitute."

"They shall be destitute no longer," replied Macpherson, jumping from his seat and blowing his whistle.

A servant appeared.

"Tell Angus Macpherson I want him."

Soon a splendid Highlander appeared. Rob Roy looked at his strongly knit frame and flashing eye with admiration.

"Angus," said Macpherson, "this is my friend, Rob Roy."

"Give me your hand, Rob Roy," exclaimed Angus, "for I like to shake hands with brave men. Your commands, my chief."

"I want you," said Macpherson, "to pick the twelve best men of the clan, and be in readiness to-morrow morning to start on an expedition."

"Very good," replied Angus, saluting as he withdrew.

"And where are the women?" asked Macpherson.

"Among the hills of Glencoe"

"With the Macdonalds?"

"The same," replied Rob Roy. "Between Ballachulish and the southern end of Lydoch. I will show your men to-morrow."

"You noble man!" exclaimed Macpherson, rising and wringing Rob Roy's hand. "I thank you from my heart. It will indeed be a blessing, for I must remain here. We expect an attack from the Robertsons any day."

"I am only too glad to be of service," replied Rob Roy.

"And when the men return with the women," said Macpherson, "I shall send a party of vengeance to visit Lydoch."

"I think," replied Rob Roy, after a pause, "it would be better to wait until I reconnoitre the ground. There are many curious things there. Strategy must be met by strategy."

"Quite true," replied Macpherson. "So be it. I shall send them when I get word from you."

CHAPTER VIII.

IN THE EAGLES' NEST.

While Rob Roy was leading the Macphersons to the relief of their women, a scene was being enacted in the Eagles' Nest Rock.

Inaccessible as the rock was outside, its appearance inside was quite different.

The rock was hollow for part of the way up, and at the bottom, enclosed by four walls of rock, sat six men.

The room, if it may be called so, was in partial darkness for the only light came through holes in the rock above.

The men were conversing in low murmurs. At the top of a rough table sat Riach with a bandaged arm. Beside him was a dark, squat, ugly, little man, with a repugnant face and jet black hair.

Next this man was a tall, dark man, with sallow complexion and scowling features, while the other three were ruffians of the worst type.

They all wore knives in their belts, and a more ruffianly lot could not be gathered together.

"I say," muttered the tall, sallow man with an oath, "that we ought to give this up. Give the swine his *conge*. Caramba! and let us put to sea."

"There is no treasure," muttered another.

"Silence!" thundered Riach, placing his pistol on the table with a bang. "At the first sign of mutiny I will blow your brains out."

"You, Recano," continued Riach,

addressing the sallow-faced man, " being a Spaniard, have no patience."

"Patience!" retorted the Spaniard, excitedly. "Patience! You talk of patience after we have been hunting a mare's nest for a year."

"An eagles' nest, you mean," interrupted the squat, little man with an ugly contortion of his face, intended for a smile.

"I say," continued Recano, not heeding the interruption, "that I am going again to sea. I do not want my share of the spoil when it is found."

"Until it is found," replied Riach, in a harsh, grating voice. "You do not leave this place alive. You might blab, and dead men tell no tales."

"Caramba!" shouted the Spaniard, in anger. "I tell you I have had enough of it. I am going to sea. Don't think you frighten me, you Scotch robber!"

Riach's eyes flashed fire. In a second there was a loud report, and the Spaniard dropped dead with a bullet through his brain.

"Cast his body into the loch," thundered Riach, as the smoke curled upwards.

The three men nearest the body rose to obey.

"Wait, wait!" exclaimed the squat, dark man. "We must not betray our secret. Wait until I go to the look out."

"Donetto is right," growled Riach. "Wait until he reports."

By this time the squat, ugly man, Donetto, was climbing up a rope ladder like a monkey. In a few minutes he reached a platform of rock that was buried in darkness.

Feeling about his hand touched another rope ladder and up it he climbed, emerging through a hole to a ledge on the outside of the rock.

Below him lay the loch, and in the distance the deserted houses of the Macphersons.

Taking a telescope from a crevice in the rock, beside which stood a nine-pounder brass carronade, evidently taken from some vessel, he carefully examined the banks of the loch and the distant hills. He saw nothing.

Almost stumbling over a mortar as he prepared to crawl through the hole, he descended below.

"There is noddings," he said with a laugh. "It is safe to use the door."

As he spoke he went to a part of the rock—or what appeared to be a part of the rock—and drew a bolt.

Pushing hard with his shoulders, a piece of the rock swung outwards.

It was an ingenious contrivance. Part of the rock had been cut clean away, while a door on which real rock was fastened had been fitted in.

From the outside detection was impossible, for the bottom of the rock was covered with green ferns, heather, and yellow broom, and on this rocky door these plants had been cunningly placed.

They were growing strong, and mixing with the other plants prevented the doorway from being seen, the outside of the door in fact being a moveable rockery or gigantic sloping flower-pot.

"Cast the body in the water!" thundered Riach, as he ominously fingered the trigger of his other pistol, "and remember disobedience is sudden death."

The ruffians took the body of their companion and cast it into the water without compunction.

"Now shut the door," growled Riach, "and to business. There is one thing," he continued, "and it is this. When you, Donetto, and your men came to me for refuge, when you were being pursued for mutiny and wrecking your ship, I gave you my protection. I took you to my cave on the other side of the loch."

"That is true," said Donetto, "and we are thankful; but I also brought you something."

"Yes," growled Riach, "but I showed you the locality. You brought news of the knowledge the Macphersons had, but I brought you to this secret place."

"But," objected Donetto, "we helped to make it."

"You helped to make it," growled Riach in return. "You helped to make this door, but," he added, fiercely, "did you make the secret passage two miles from here, leading from this spot to the hills."

"No," replied Donetto, losing his temper, "neither did you. It is natural."

"It is natural," grunted Riach; "but where, in the name of all the fiends, would one suspect there was such a place."

"True," replied Donetto, "but we brought our cannon, and our mortar, and our ammunition, and our carcasses from the ship."

"And I showed you the way," roared Riach, in a rage. "Enough of this. You promised to obey me until we found the treasure. Then you, Donetto, and I were to have one-half between us, and the rest divided between the others. Am I, or am I not, to continue your chief."

"If not," he roared, as he flourished his pistol, viciously in the air, "if not I blow every one of your cursed brains out now."

The men shrank back afraid of him, for, indeed, he looked a demon incarnate.

"There is no question," said Donetto, in a soothing voice, but with hatred burning in his eyes. "There is no question. We are all angry because the chart is lost."

"It is not lost!" shouted Riach. "I tell you it is in the Eagles' Nest."

Donetto shrugged his shoulders.

"I tell you it is," growled Riach, who was in a fearful temper, and looking for a row. "You need not shrug your shoulders. I tell you it is."

"I believe you, my friend."

"Don't friend me," yelled Riach, "I tell you it is there, and has been for the past nine months. I took it out on the ledge to refresh my memory, in the broad daylight, when one of the eagles swooped down and carried it off."

The men did not speak, but beneath their cunning looks a keen observer could see that they did not believe him.

"And since that time we cannot extract any information from the prisoner," said Donetto, breaking the silence.

"And we cannot cut our way up to the eyrie," said one of the men, suddenly finding his voice.

"And we cannot climb it from outside," added another, emboldened by his comrade's speech.

"No," rejoined the third man, "for the rock slopes outwards from the base."

"Let us try the prisoner once more," said Donetto.

Riach stared moodily at the rocky wall.

"Let us have some whisky first," he grunted. "Quick, fetch a fresh supply."

In a moment the three men ran to a corner, and disappeared down a long flight of narrow steps hewn out of the rock. In a few minutes they emerged into daylight that shone on them from overhead.

They stood in a remarkable place. As far as the eye could reach was a long streak of light overhead that was reflected below on a rushing stream.

At one time this stream had run on the ground many feet above its present bed, but through long ages had worn away the sandy rocks which had apparently been soft in the centre of the stream.

The result was that for some two miles a large tunnel open at the top for some two feet ran under the Eagles' Nest Rock from the mountains to the loch, this crack in the earth being completely hidden by the rocks above ground that were thrown together in tumultous confusion for hundreds of yards on either side of the subterranean river.

But the men did not pause to gaze on the scene of rugged beauty. They hastened along the footpath they had helped to make until they came to a wider part of the cavernous passage.

There on a plot of thick green grass and bracken lay the four stolen carts tipped on their ends as if cast down a hole.

Quickly filling their horn flagons, they returned to the room in the rock.

"Taken a year about nothing," growled Riach, tossing a quaich or horn cupful of fiery liquid down his throat. "Come, Donetto, let us tackle the prisoner again."

CHAPTER IX.

CHAINED TO THE ROCK.

As he spoke, Riach climbed up the rope ladder, followed by Donetto.

Gaining the first ledge, he struck a light and lit a torch, fixing it in a crevice of the rock.

The uncertain flickering light threw itself over a ghastly sight.

It was evidently a man, or had been a man at one time of strong build.

His eyes, appearing on his sallow, shrunken face below a mass of matted, tangled hair that lay in lumps on his shoulders, glowed like live coal. His beard hung down to his waist.

His form was bent almost double, and his skinny knees protruded through the wretched rags that hung about his limbs.

His bare ankles were encircled with rusty iron chains that were attached to gyves on his wrists, and bound him securely to the rock.

By his side on a ledge was a discarded lump of oat cake and a horn of water.

He glared fiercely at his persecutors, who regarded him in silence.

"Ha!" he croaked in hoarse, gutteral sounds. "Ha! you come once more to torture me, but I shall carry the secret to the grave!"

"Fool," hissed Riach. "For nigh upon one year you have been bearing a living death. Once more I ask you to reveal the secret. What were the number of paces, and what the direction?"

The figure chuckled like a madman.

"You, Riach the robber, and you, Donetto, the murderer and false friend, thought that by murdering my brothers who held the secret with me, you could force me, the only one who knew it, to divulge it. You attacked me, stunned, and carried me hence. Then you murdered my brothers; but never, never shall I tell."

"Once more," roared Riach, irritated at the croaking of the prisoner, "once more, are you going to consent. We shall set you free."

"What is freedom to me now?" said the prisoner in a hoarse whisper, while his eyes blazed with madness. "What is freedom to me? Ask the eagles."

Riach winced under the thrust.

"Ask the eagles," repeated the prisoner. "They have the secret in their safe keeping."

"Put a bullet through his head," sneered Donetto. "He is useless to us."

"No, no," replied Riach; "with his death the secret dies with him, and then we are lost."

"We might find it ourselves."

"We might," re-echoed Riach, with fine scorn, "we might and so might Loch Lydoch run dry."

Turning to the prisoner, Riach said:

"Think over it. Torture we have tried, and torture we shall try again. Think over it, and if you do not speak in a few days' time when I return I will torture you to the brink of the grave."

"Do your worst, you fiend," retorted the prisoner. "Fergus Macpherson, while he draws breath, fears no foe."

CHAPTER X.

CHECKMATED.

When Rob Roy bade farewell to the Macphersons as they turned homewards with the widows and children, he waited until dusk.

When darkness set in he set out for the deserted houses near Loch Lydoch.

As he approached the loch he started with surprise, for all of a sudden specks of light appeared on the rock of the Eagles' Nest.

"It is a puzzle," he muttered, as he stood and gazed at the rock. "Ah," he added, "I have it. That rock is hollow, and doubtless is the abode of the ruffians. I was inclined to think it was but a place for observation, but how they could climb it beats me. Now, I see. It is hollow. So much more of an advance towards the punishment of these brutes."

But Rob Roy was not particularly interested in the rock at the present time. He had another object in view.

Cautiously going to the deserted house he had already visited, he listened for a few minutes until satisfied that no one was within.

Pushing open the door, he felt his way towards the fireplace, and was gratified to find that his Macpherson disguise had not been taken away.

"That shows," he muttered, "that they do not suspect as yet."

Taking the bundle, he silently left the house, and retraced his steps the way he came. In a few hours he arrived at the houses just vacated by the women.

Throwing some dry heather in a corner of the room, he flung himself down, and was soon fast alseep.

He was up before the sun next morning, and donning the Macpherson tartan, started off for Ballachulish.

The fishermen and others connected with the several boats that called there were standing about their cottages when Rob Roy entered the village.

"Good morning to you, sir," said Rob Roy, cheerily to the first fisherman he met.

"Good morning to you, sir," replied the fisherman; "and who might ye be wanting."

"To tell you the truth," replied Rob Roy, "I am setting up in one of the houses at Lydoch, and may be you could tell me where I could buy a couple of chairs, a table, and some things like that."

"That I can," answered the man, staring hard at Rob Roy, "but surely ye must be mad to think o' setting up there."

"Why ? "

"Why, man, may the Lord be good to us ! A Macpherson asking such a question when the houses are red with his clan's blood."

"That I know," said Rob Roy, slowly, "but there, I am going to go."

"I think, then, that the Macphersons are all bewitched," replied the man.

"Never mind that. It may be and it may not be. Where can I get the things I asked."

"Oh, from Rory of the Plane. He's the village carpenter and boatwright. The second house east of the third house west of here."

Rob Roy thanked the man and followed the directions.

Rory of the Plane was busy with his boats, and at the same time was conversing with a squat, ugly man in seafaring clothes, no other than Donetto himself.

"I tell you, man," exclaimed Rory, with emphasis, "I saw the man mysel'. He was a Macpherson right enough and said he was going to take up his quarters at Lydoch."

"Oh," replied Donetto, "it is nothing to me, only if a Macpherson or anyone else was going there I should be sorry."

"For why ? "

"Because I want the rafters of the houses to help to make a boat for me, and if anyone came I could not take them. At present they are rotting."

"But surely you could get your village joiner to make a boat."

"No," replied the cunning Donetto. "Our village is twelve miles down the coast. There is no wood, and, what is more, there is no wright like Rory of the Plane."

Rory laughed with pleasure. At that moment a shadow crossed the doorway.

"As I am a living man," he exclaimed, "here is the very Macpherson I was talking of."

Donetto's eyes twinkled as Rob Roy made his request.

"That can be easily done," said Rory of the Plane, "and some of the men could bear a hand to carry them."

"With pleasure," interjected Donetto.

"Although I come from a village far down the coast I should be pleased, for I have nothing to do for a few days until my boat is mended."

"But you are not a Highlander," said Rob Roy, eyeing the man up and down.

Donetto lowered his eyes before Rob Roy's piercing gaze.

"Ah, no," he exclaimed, with a greasy smile. "I have not that pleasure. I am but a poor Spaniard, who was wrecked off the coast many years ago. Your countrymen treated me well, and I am one of them now."

"Liar," thought Rob Roy. "The man's an Italian, but the one is as bad as the other. I'll keep my eye on you, my hearty."

Rob Roy, with much ostentation, bought provisions, some furniture, and several articles of clothing.

He was the cynosure of all eyes, and the talk of the village, and no one tried to ingratiate himself more than Donetto.

In a few hours Rob Roy was ready to start, and Donetto would take no denial. He would help.

"I may be mistaken after all," thought Rob Roy. "I did not like his looks at first, but he is a pleasant fellow."

"Well," said Rob Roy, "if you will help me, kindly oblige me by telling me to whom I am indebted."

"Alfonso Blanco," was the unblushing reply.

"Very well, friend Alfonso, we will start now. I think we can manage between us."

"Yes, yes," replied Donetto, with alacrity.

Donetto managed occasionally to lag behind, but Rob Roy was too accomplished a Highlander and campaigner to allow such tactics in a stranger, particularly in the narrow mountain passes.

"I am going too fast," said Rob Roy, apologetically. "You go first, for I fancy I am the stronger man, and I'll take my pace from you."

Donetto smiled an oily smile, but his eyes shot hate.

Well it was that Rob Roy did so, for more than once Donetto's hand stole towards his stiletto, ready to strike the gallant chieftain down at the first opportunity.

Despite Donetto's manœuvres to fall behind, Rob Roy would have none of it, and at length they arrived at Loch Lydoch.

"What rock is that?" asked Donetto. "It looks curious."

"I have not had much time to examine it," replied Rob Roy, casually—which was true.

"But why, may I ask," queried Donetto, "do you choose to live here when you do not know the district?"

"I am a hunter," replied Rob Roy. "There are many red deer in the forests or the hills beyond, and there are many others in the rivers. When I gather sufficient skins I send them to Glasgow."

"Wonderful!" exclaimed Donetto. "What a life of adventure it must be!"

"Very quiet," replied Rob Roy; "and besides, I wish to be here to practise shooting. To tell you the truth, I am a bad shot, and am laughed at at home; but when I return I shall take my place with the best."

"Ha, ha, ha!" laughed Donetto, uproariously. "I should like to see your comrades when you return. There is plenty of room to learn here."

"There is, friend," replied Rob Roy. "Now to set the house in order."

They placed the table and two chairs in the centre of the room, and Donetto's eyes gleamed with a cunning light when they put the bed up in the corner opposite the door.

Donetto measured the distance with his eye. He had only to slip in at night and give the Macpherson his *conge*.

"When I settle down," said Rob Roy, "my good friend, Alfonso, you must come and stay with me for a few days for fishing and shooting."

"The very thing," exclaimed Donetto. "I shall be delighted. Now I must be going. No, I insist. I can find my way back all right. My dear friend, it will take you all your time to set your house in order."

And in a moment Donetto was gone.

"Slippery fish," muttered Rob Roy, as he watched Donetto disappear among the hills. "It will never do to let Italians or Spaniards roam about here. I shall see him a little further."

Rob Roy quickly left the house, and keeping in the shadow of the thick bushes of broom took a circuitous route to catch Donetto in the flank. From the hills he could then see Donetto's movements.

When Rob Roy arrived at the side of the pass through which Donetto had to go, he saw no trace of him. Rob Roy knew that he had not time to be there already, so he moved cautiously in the direction of the loch.

Suddenly he stopped. A movement on the face of the hills opposite attracted his attention, and soon he saw "his dear friend Alfonso" emerge from the broom and waving bracken.

Donetto crawled to the top of the mountain which was one overlooking the loch and the houses, and exactly opposite the Rock of the Eagles' Nest.

When he gained the top he fixed his eyes on the houses, and seeing no sign outside he crawled down the hill for a few yards, and rising up sped quickly onwards.

Circling round the loch he dodged under the shadow of the rocks, and scrambling over them he touched a spring and a chasm opened above the roaring torrent. Below him were the carts and casks.

Descending steps cut out of the face of the rock, he pulled a lever and the wood-work with the painted rocks on it closed the hole at once.

With breathless haste he made for the room at the bottom of the rock.

As he ran up the steps he almost collided with Riach, who stood at the top gloomily with his arms folded.

"What fur!" he shouted. "I helped the new-comer, Macpherson, to fit up his house. He is green."

"Macpherson!" repeated Riach, in scathing tones. "Macpherson! You cursed fool, he is no Macpherson. He is Rob Roy MacGregor. I watched him through the glass, and there is only one man like him, and that is himself."

Donetto was taken aback.

"Anyway," he muttered under his breath after a while, "to-night he shall die."

Rob Roy meanwhile made a detour and gained his house unnoticed.

"And so," he muttered, "my good friend, Alfonso, is Donetto, the murderer. I thought so from the very first."

CHAPTER XI.

A MIDNIGHT ASSASSIN.

It had been dark for some hours when a lithe form glided from the rock of the Eagles' Nest.

It cautiously skirted the edge of the loch and paused before the deserted houses of the Macphersons.

The night was clear, and the bright starlight reflected on something gleaming the figure carried in its right hand.

The gleaming object was the glass dagger of Donetto as the murderer crept forward to accomplish his fiendish design.

Donetto reached the door of Rob Roy's house and listened intently.

Rob Roy was asleep, and the murderer could hear his heavy breathing.

Donetto waited until he made sure his victim was asleep, then he quietly lifted the latch and pushed the door open.

Rob Roy's recumbent form was darkly outlined on the rude bed in the corner of the room.

Thither Donetto, crouching like a panther, stealthily advanced.

The dagger flashed on high and instantly buried itself in the breast of the victim.

"Donetto, the murderer!"

The words rang out like a trumpet peal. Donetto screamed with terror and attempted to rush from the house.

But the cold steel of a pistol pressed against his brow made him stagger back.

"Donetto, you are my prisoner!"

It was Rob Roy who spoke, as he stepped from behind the door.

Quickly shutting the door, Rob Roy lit a fir candle and set it on the table.

The terror-stricken Donetto was cringing in a corner, his teeth chattering. The man he thought he had murdered stood before him covering him with a pistol.

"Hold your hands above your head!" thundered Rob Roy.

The cowering wretch did as he was told, and Rob Roy quickly disarmed him by taking a couple of pistols from his belt and a stiletto from the folds of his over-shirt.

"You see," laughed Rob Roy, "I have come prepared," and taking a piece of stout cord from the table he quickly bound his prisoner.

"Look, you murderer," said Rob Roy, sternly, as he undid the bundle of clothing on the bed that had done duty for his body, "look, you murderer, how you were foiled."

Donetto was too much taken aback to reply. He was at heart an arrant coward, and he had not yet recovered from the shock of the terrible words that suddenly rang out in the darkness—

"Donetto, the murderer!"

"Listen to me," ordered Rob Roy, "and first let me sit you down on a chair."

Rob Roy lifted Donetto and dumped him down on a chair.

"Now, listen to me and answer truly."

"Spare my life! Spare my life!" whined the wretched man.

"Yes," retorted Rob Roy, fiercely, "as you spared the innocent Macphersons when you took their lives in the dead of the night, and spared the feelings of the widows and children."

Donetto cowered before Rob Roy's fierce gaze.

"Answer my questions!" thundered the irate chieftain.

"Have you found the treasure?" demanded Rob Roy.

"I should not be there if we had," returned Donetto, telling the truth for once.

"Why have you not found it?" asked Rob Roy. "You have got the chart."

Donetto started as if stabbed.

"You know all," he muttered. "We have not got the chart."

"Why is that?"

"Because Riach says that the eagles carried it off one day as he went outside the rock to examine the figures carefully in daylight."

"But he can remember the figures, surely?"

"No, he does not. He thought he did at first. Then he was not certain, and we have been digging everywhere."

"And have found nothing?"

"No, we have not."

"Were you the man I knocked against in the dark the other day?"

"I was."

"How did it happen you were crossing the loch at that time of night."

"I had been spying at Ballachulish, and the nearest way is across the loch. Riach keeps a boat at the other side by the cave he used to live in."

"Why were you going back?"

"I was not going back. I was going to moor the boat, which I had forgotten."

"How did you enter the rock?"

"By the secret door."

"Where is it?"

"On the north side of the rock. It is an artificial door. It is covered outside with broom and bracken. We know it because two large broom bushes grow on it."

" How does it open ? "

" By pushing it outwards."

" Can it be opened from the outside ? "

" Not unless the bolt inside is un-barred, and the door left slightly ajar."

" Then the opening of the door accounts for the flash of light that heralded your approach ? "

" Yes. I expect so."

" How many other entrances are there ? "

" Two."

" Where are they ? "

" One is two miles away, hidden among the rocks where the stream rushes down the mountain side, and apparently goes underneath the ground."

" You say ' apparently.' Why is that ? "

" Because the stream has burrowed underground, and has dug out a huge tunnel with a rent on the top. Flowers and grass grow in this tunnel, which is really an arbour."

" Why cannot one see any signs of it from above ? "

" Because no one has the patience to climb over hundreds of yards of sharp-pointed rocks."

" Then how did you get the carts over those rocks ? "

" We did not get them over the rocks."

" Well, how did you spirit them away ? "

" There is another entrance."

" The second one you mentioned ? "

" Yes."

" Where is it ? "

" Only some fifty yards from the bend of the road by the loch side."

" Is it easily seen ? "

" No. It is really a trap-door, which acts as a roof to an off-shoot of the tunnel I spoke of. There is a secret spring under the first large stone on the shingle before you come to the rocks."

" Yes, I know. The stretch of pebble between the roadway and the rocks."

" This trap-door is made of wood, and is roughly painted, besides rough shingle being glued on to it."

" It must be easily seen," said Rob Roy.

" You could not see it," retorted Donetto.

" Did you see us searching ? "

" Yes. From the look-out."

" Where is that ? "

" On a ledge a few feet below the Eagles' nest."

" But about this trap-door arrange-ment ? "

" The spring is under the stone. One-half of this stone is grey, the other half black. When you press the spring the door falls downwards. Stone steps lead below, and on the grass at the bottom stands the handle of a lever. This acts on a rope, and shuts the entrance."

" Did you murder all the Mac-phersons ? "

Donetto made no reply.

" Answer my question. The Mac-phersons were stabbed with a glass stiletto of Italian make. Were you the murderer ? "

" Not of them all."

" Of how many ? "

" Six."

" Who murdered the seventh ? "

" He is not dead."

" Not dead ! " exclaimed Rob Roy, " where is he ? "

" In the rock."

" A prisoner ? "

" Yes."

" Why is he kept alive ? "

" Because he knows the secret of the lost chart."

" Then to kill him would be to spoil all ? "

" Yes."

Rob Roy watched Donetto closely. There was a curious gleam in his eye.

" He is trying to gain time," thought Rob Roy, as he strained his ears.

" Donetto," he said, " you may, or you may not, expect assistance from your fellow robbers, but I say this to you, that on the first attempt at rescue or escape I shall blow out your brains where you stand."

Donetto looked crestfallen.

Suddenly Rob Roy heard a slight noise outside, and immediately the door was burst open, and several shots were fired into the room.

Rob Roy at once returned fire. Donetto wriggled to his feet, and at that moment a stray shot knocked the candle over and plunged the house in darkness.

The robbers made a rush for the door-way, and in an instant Rob Roy's claymore leapt from its scabbard.

With one mighty sweep Rob Roy cut down the foremost man.

" Come on, you murderers," he shouted " you shall all share the same fate."

But the death of the first man stopped the rush, and as Rob Roy sprang forward with a shout they took to their heels and ran. They knew the danger of being within reach of the Highland chieftain's sword.

"It is useless to pursue them further," muttered Rob Roy, as he turned towards the house.

Suddenly his quick eye caught a dark object by the doorway. He spurned it with his foot. It was soft and yielding.

"Ah, my noble murderer," he exclaimed in deep sarcasm. "So you thought you would escape, did you? You have done well to wriggle this far."

Saying so, Rob Roy seized him and carried him into the house. Lighting the candle, he said, sternly:

"Donetto, your hands are red with innocent blood, and the longer you live the redder they would get. It would ill befit me to take your life without warning. In ten minutes you die. Look at these walls stained with the life's blood of men. Make your peace, for in ten minutes you die."

Donetto whined and fumed in turns; then suddenly he became calm. His quick ear had detected sounds outside.

Rob Roy heard the noise, and quick as lightning he stuck his bonnet on Donetto's head.

Through the open window came a blinding flash, followed by the hurried step of someone running away.

When the smoke cleared away Donetto lay face downwards on the table, shot through the head.

"'Tis a just punishment," muttered Rob Roy, "and a case of dog eat dog. This house is not safe to-night, and my better plan is to hurry home and get the help of my gallant clansmen."

Quickly dressing in his own clothes, Rob Roy loaded his pistols, and saw to the priming, and slinging his targe on his back, strode out into the darkness, sword in hand.

CHAPTER XII.

A Dangerous Game.

When Rob Roy left the house he intended to make straight for Balquhidder and get the assistance of some of his clansmen, but he recollected that there was a prisoner in the rock and that that prisoner could be no other than Fergus Macpherson.

Rob Roy's noble heart was at once touched by the thought of the sufferings of the unfortunate man at the hands of the ruffians, and he at once determined to attempt a rescue.

Knowing that in the darkness it was worse than useless to try to find the entrance in the rocks, he set off at once for the distant hills, taking care to keep close to the ragged stretch of rocks that ran towards the foot of the hills.

After an arduous walk he reached the hills and heard the gurgling of the stream as it rushed down the mountain side.

Carefully feeling his way towards it, he was overjoyed when his feet accidently trod on a footpath.

"This is the right track at the offset," he muttered to himself. "It is too wide for a goat-track, and must be the one Donetto mentioned had been made by the gang."

The path led downwards, and by the hollow sound of his footsteps Rob Roy knew that he was in the tunnel.

Keeping close to the rocks, he walked cautiously along until he found his way barred by a flight of stone steps.

"This must lead into the stronghold," said Rob Roy, as he began to ascend.

Soon he discerned the faint glimmer of a light, and the hum of voices smote his ears.

Rob Roy stood still, ready to fight to the bitter end.

"I tell you I killed him," said a voice. "I just got a glimpse of his head, and I saw him fall forward on the table when I fired."

"All right," grunted Riach, in a sleepy voice. "Get to bed. We shall see in the morning."

Rob Roy grasped his claymore more firmly, but the man did not descend. Instead of that, he threw himself on some heather in a corner of the room.

Rob Roy crept forward, and his eyes came level with the floor. Four men, he saw, were lying down, while beyond them he could see a rope-ladder dangling from above.

"The prisoner must be upstairs," muttered Rob Roy, "and I must rescue him at all costs; for if I make an attack afterwards they will put him to death."

For a long time Rob Roy waited, and at last all the men were snoring loudly.

Rob Roy was tempted to run his sword through the gullet of each, but the idea was repugnant to the heroic chieftain.

Threading his way to the ladder, he ascended and found himself in darkness.

A faint moan startled him.

"The prisoner," he muttered. "But where is he? I must not shout."

Again the faint moan struck his ears.

Feeling about with his hands in the darkness, Rob Roy grasped another rope-ladder.

"He may be up above," he said to himself, as he began to climb.

The ladder ended abruptly on a sharp ledge. Feeling his way forward he was struck on the face by a cold blast of air.

The passage he felt he was in narrowed, and bending down he crawled through an aperture and beheld the stars.

By their dim light he saw the mortar and the carronade.

His first impulse was to heave the thing over the face of the rock, but on second thoughts he remembered that the noise would waken the ruffians below.

"The prisoner must be down below," he said, after he had examined the ledge. "I shall descend."

As he climbed downwards, the faint moan again struck his ears. Without hesitation Rob Roy struck a light, and was horror-struck at the sight that met his gaze.

Hollow-eyed, in rags and tatters, and shrunken to a mere skeleton, Fergus MacPherson stood before him.

The poor man gazed unintelligently at Rob Roy.

"My God!" muttered Rob Roy, with tears in his eyes. "It is terrible. He has lost his reason."

And so it was. Fergus Macpherson, once the gallant, strong man, looked at Rob Roy with the vacant stare of absolute idiocy. His terrible sufferings had at last told on his unconquerable spirit.

Rob Roy's blood boiled, and he turned to descend the rope-ladder and fall upon the ruffians.

As he did so, his claymore struck the rocks with a loud clang.

In a second the ruffians sprang to their feet.

Escape was impossible, for they were in the room below, and barred the only exits from the rock.

"Who's there?" demanded Riach.

Rob Roy made no answer.

"The noise came from above," said Riach. "Go," he added, addressing one of the men, "and see what it proceeds from."

The man climbed up the ladder, and as he gained the top he caught sight of Rob Roy ready to cut him down.

He gave a yell and fell off the ladder on to the top of his companions.

"What is it?" roared Riach, dragging the man to his feet. "What is it?"

"The ghost of Rob Roy, the man I shot to-night," whispered the man in awe-struck tones. "It has got a sword in its hand."

"Ghost be hanged," roared Riach. "I shall soon see."

Running up the ladder at a furious pace, Riach was on the rocky platform in a moment, and before he knew where he was he was seized by the collar by a strong hand.

But Riach was a powerful man and no small weight. With a wrench he tore himself free, for Rob Roy could only use his left hand, his claymore being in his right.

So much exertion had Riach put forward that he left part of his hunting deerskin coat in Rob Roy's hand, and when the garment gave way he was precipitated into the room below.

"Curse you, Rob Roy," he yelled, as he toppled backwards. "Curse you," he again roared, as he rose to his feet. "You are my prisoner, and ha! ha! there is no escape."

To descend amongst the ruffians was quite out of the question, for Rob Roy would have been cut to pieces before he reached the ground. So he stood for a moment and contemplated his position.

While he stood Riach shouted up to him.

"Rob Roy, step to the front. I wish to speak to you."

"I am perfectly comfortable here," replied Rob Roy, as he stood well away from the top of the ladder in case any of the ruffians should take it into their heads to fire at him.

Riach uttered an oath at Rob Roy's answer.

"You are my prisoner," he yelled.

"So you remarked before," replied Rob Roy, coolly.

"And you have got to die," roared Riach.

"Every man has got to die once, and once only," said Rob Roy, calmly.

"Yes," exclaimed Riach, savagely, "and your once will come very soon."

"It will come at the proper time," replied Rob Roy, with irritating tranquillity.

"We will starve you out," shouted Riach. "That will be a better death for you."

"I shall help you," exclaimed Rob Roy, suddenly bending forward and seizing the end of the rope-ladder.

With a powerful jerk he pulled the ladder up to the platform.

"That will prevent them interfering with my plans," he said. "Now to release this poor fellow."

The rusty iron bands had eaten into his cankered skin, for flesh he had none, and so rusty was the iron that Rob Roy found it impossible to undo the bands.

Taking his dirk, he hacked at the cement that held the chains in the wall, and after a quarter of an hour's hard work he succeeded in detaching the fetters from the wall.

Meanwhile Fergus stood docile and vacant-eyed. The poor creature could scarcely move. He had forgotten how to use his limbs.

Rob Roy thought for a moment. Winding the rope-ladder round his waist, Rob Roy lifted Fergus, chains and all, in his strong arms and ascended the rope-ladder above.

Placing Fergus on the rocky platform, Rob Roy crawled through the aperture, pulling Fergus after him.

Then he crawled back and pulled up the rope-ladder.

The fresh air revived Fergus somewhat, and Rob Roy, taking off his plaid and doublet, dressed Fergus in the latter and wound the plaid round him.

"Do you know me, Fergus? I am Rob Roy," said Rob Roy, bending down and speaking kindly.

A gleam of intelligence shot into Fergus' eyes, and he moved his jaws as if to speak. But his tongue refused to move. It was parched dry.

Rob Roy looked hastily around; then he knelt down and peered over the ledge of the rock.

In the dim morning light he saw that the distance was great.

"It may do," he muttered. "I'll try, anyway."

Joining the two rope-ladders together, he cast it over the ledge.

Again he bent down and peered over to ascertain the length of the rope.

As he did so a harsh, brutal laugh sounded from below. The rope was several yards short, and the ruffians laughed until the tears came into their eyes.

"It matters little now," said Rob Roy, "for they know my plan, and they will be on the watch."

Riach and his fellow-ruffians kept shouting from below, but Rob Roy could only hear dull sounds; the distance was too great.

Half a day passed, and Rob Roy kept a sharp look-out both on the enemy and for any stranger that might happen to pass.

As he sat thinking over several plans, he suddenly leapt to his feet and put his hand to his ear.

Then he gave a wild shout.

"'Tis the slogan of the MacGregors," he cried, and listened intently.

Nearer and nearer came the stirring strains. The ruffians heard it and shut themselves up in the rock.

Rob Roy shaded his eyes with his hand and gazed in the direction of the distant hills from whence the sounds came.

Again he gave another shout.

Swinging round the base of the mountain two miles away was a body of kilted men, and by the slogan Rob Roy knew that they were MacGregors.

On they came until they halted some 500 yards away.

"I see Alastair, my brother, and I see Davidson and Big John," exclaimed Rob Roy. "Fergus," he cried, turning to his companion, "we are saved."

When the MacGregors came to a halt, Rob Roy put his hands to his mouth, and gave vent to a scream like the curlew.

He saw the MacGregors start and stare at the rock, and in a moment Alastair answered the signal.

Rob Roy then took the plaid from Fergus, and waved it wildly. Davidson saw it, and pointed towards the rock.

The order for the advance was given, and until Rob Roy remembered that the ruffians could not climb up to their loop-holes he wondered why they did not open fire.

The MacGregors were now within easy distance of recognition, and Rob Roy pointed warningly downwards with his finger.

Alastair and Davidson waved their hands to say that they understood.

Rob Roy then drew from his bosom an old letter, and tearing open the envelope wrote hastily. Tying the letter to a stone he flung it over the rock.

Alastair picked it up and read.

"Send men to guard entrance two

miles away at foot of hills. Watch where carts disappeared. Surround the rock ; four men inside. Get Donald the archer to fire the arrow with string attached over the rock, and I shall pull up rope.''

The orders were instantly obeyed.

" There," said Davidson, in answer to a question from Alastair, " this is about the spot where the carts disappeared."

Suddenly Donald the archer sent an arrow whizzing with unerring aim over the rock, and Rob Roy at once grabbed the string.

Pulling at it, he gradually hauled up a huge length of the smugglers' ropes.

Making signs that he had some one with him Rob Roy fastened the ropes round Fergus's body, and gently lowered him to the ground.

" My God !" exclaimed Davidson " what mystery is this ? It is Fergus Macpherson or his ghost !"

But there was no time for inquiry.

" Take good care of him, men," said Davidson to his smugglers. " Keep him warm in the meantime, and give him a drink."

Having pulled up the rope again, Rob Roy made it fast, and descended with lightning speed to the ground.

He was plied with questions and congratulations.

" What adventure is this, Rob ? " asked Alastair, with a laugh.

" I'll tell you afterwards. There is no time to be lost."

At that moment a shout long and loud rose from the hills.

" 'Tis the MacGregor's war cry," said Rob Roy. " Come, let us go. They have tracked the ruffians."

The MacGregors rushed forward, but they were too late to be in at the death, for the advance party had fallen on the fleeing ruffians as they left the tunnel, and cut them to pieces with their claymores.

" Now for the chart," said Rob Roy.

" What chart ? " exclaimed Alastair and Davidson.

" Oh ! I forgot," replied Rob Roy, " I shall tell you after."

" Donald," said Rob Roy, " shoot an arrow with string over the very top of the rock, and be quick for the eagles will soon be back."

Donald shot the arrow, and Rob Roy ran round to the other side of the rock, and secured the string.

" Fasten rope on it," he called.

This was done, and immediately the rope was hauled over the cliff, and made secure.

Rob Roy then ascended the first rope to the ledge, from whence he climbed up the second rope to the Eagles' Nest.

His search was brief, for among the sticks that made the nest the first thing he saw was a piece of parchment.

It was the missing chart.

Seeing the eagles in the distance Rob Roy made a hasty descent.

" When we get home I shall tell you the story," he said ; " but first of all we must see to Fergus Macpherson, and we must keep the carronade and mortar that are now on the ledge above."

The carronade and mortar were soon secured.

" Davidson, I have a surprise for you," said Rob Roy. " Your carts are safe."

Taking Davidson to the grey and black stone, Rob Roy touched the spring. The door opened, and there the carts, none the worse, met Davidson's astonished gaze.

" You are a most remarkable man," exclaimed Davidson. " The most remarkable I ever knew," which was a big speech for Davidson.

" We shall encamp here until Macpherson's wife arrives," said Rob Roy, and so they did.

The meeting between Fergus and his wife was most pathetic, but under her careful nursing he soon regained his strength, and became the most talked-about man in the Macpherson clan.

A long time afterwards, when he had entirely recovered, the treasure was dug up and distributed among the poor, much to the delight of Rob Roy, who made the suggestion.

The secret door of the Rock of the Eagles' Nest was destroyed, as also was the trap-door arrangement among the rocks, the only habitable place that was left being the Eagles' Nest.

THE END.

Published by JAMES HENDERSON AND SONS at Red Lion House, Red Lion-court, Fleet-street, E.C.

www.ingramcontent.com/pod-product-compliance
Lightning Source LLC
Chambersburg PA
CBHW082054220626
47052CB00006B/1231